Bradley
The New Forest Bear

Contents

Page 3

Story 1 Bradley to the Rescue

Bradley the little grey New Forest bear was playing in the garden. It was summertime. He had many brothers and sisters, all colours and sizes. They played together, sometimes indoors but mostly in the garden. It was a wonderful summer with long warm days full of butterflies and bird song. Bradley loved the trees and flowers and the little animals he met in the garden. The squirrels always made him laugh.

Page 4

In the house lived a very old brown bear who wore a battered old black hat. He had only one eye and some of the stuffing had fallen out of his legs, so he was a little bit wobbly. He knew all the plants by name. Seeing Bradley's interest in them he started to teach him. One day Bradley and the old bear were in the garden, it was nearly the end of summer. "You know Bradley," said the old bear, "I think the job that you would like would be to work in the forest." "Would I have to go away?" asked Bradley. "Yes, but not far. You can always come and visit, I will always be here if you need me." The old bear knew the young bears would soon be sold. "I will be sad to see you go Bradley," said the old bear. "Somehow, I have the feeling that YOU are very special."

As the days became colder Bradley and his brothers and sisters spent more time indoors. One day they were playing Hide and Seek, Bradley ran into the hall. There, piled high, were some very large cardboard boxes. Bradley lifted the lid of a box and jumped in to hide. Then he heard voices. "We must pack all the bears into the boxes tonight and we must start early tomorrow morning." "Goodness," thought Bradley, "what will tomorrow bring?" When Bradley was found he told the others what he had heard. The young bears gathered together feeling rather sad. "I'm sure we will meet again sometime," said one bear. "What if we are not loved?" said one of his sisters. "We will be, all bears are loved," said Bradley. A few moments later they were all packed into the waiting boxes.

In the morning the boxes were lifted into the car, the engine started and they were off. It seemed as if they were travelling for a long time. When the car stopped Bradley lifted the lid of the box and peeped out. He could see a sign saying Alderholt Craft Fair. The boxes were carried into the hall and unpacked. The bears were brushed to look their best and put up for sale. People came and looked at the bears and some of Bradley's family were sold. Suddenly Bradley was chosen and went to live in Lymington with a kind lady. She lived all alone in a little white cottage with a green door and roses all around. Bradley's love of the New Forest grew stronger. He was always up in the morning before the sun, to make sure the forest was clean and tidy for the visitors. One morning he heard a tiny cry "Help! Help! Oh please help me!" He moved towards the sound. A short distance on he found a tin can. Trapped inside was his friend Mrs Hedgehog. She had been looking for food and gone into the tin. She was trapped by the sharp edges and could not get out. "Stay still," said Bradley, "I'll force the can open, then maybe you can manage to scramble free."

Bradley pushed his walking stick into the can and tried to lever it open. It took all his strength. He pulled and pulled until finally out popped Mrs Hedgehog. Oh what a sorry sight. Her little neck was badly cut. "Have you been in there all night?" said Bradley. "Yes, from the time the moon came up," said Mrs Hedgehog. Bradley took off his scarf and wrapped it round Mrs Hedgehog to keep her warm, as she was feeling very cold. "I must get her to hospital," Bradley thought, "Can you manage to walk a little way? Here, use my stick." Bradley took Mrs Hedgehog's other paw and helped her to walk. "Now wait here by this log and I will run and get my car."

Very soon they arrived at Lymington Hospital. Bradley told the doctor what had happened. The doctor examined Mrs Hedgehog very carefully. "Well done, Bradley. You kept her nice and warm she is going to be all right." The nurses took great care of Mrs Hedgehog and fitted a comfortable bandage. Then Bradley took Mrs Hedgehog home. All their friends came to meet them. One mouse brought cakes and biscuits and another some lemonade. Mrs Rabbit spread a blue checked tablecloth on the ground and they all had a party to celebrate that Mrs Hedgehog was going to be all right. After Mrs Hedgehog had eaten her meal she said, "Thank you all for this lovely party. What with the excitement this morning, and all this delicious food, I am feeling sleepy. So if you don't mind I'll just have a little nap." She then curled up under a nearby hedge and fell fast asleep.

The other animals didn't mind at all. When it was time to clear everything away they were very careful to put the rubbish into the dustbin. After all, they would not want someone else to have an accident.

Bradley clears up the Garden.

Story 2   Bradley Visits Milford-on-Sea

Bradley the little grey New Forest bear arrived in Milford early one morning. It was the Spring Bank Holiday. There were people already working on the Village Green putting up tents, tables and flags. There was to be a Fair on the Green that afternoon, with a Merry-Go-Round, Competitions and dancing round the Maypole. "I'll help," said Bradley and started work eagerly. Everything was soon ready.

Now Bradley had a friend in the village, called Snowy. He had invited him to come and stay for a holiday. When Bradley arrived, he told Snowy that he had been helping on the Green. There was to be a Fancy Dress Competition and Dancing round the Maypole. Snowy became very excited and said, "Shall we enter the Fancy Dress Competition?" "What shall we go as?" asked Bradley. "While we have lunch we will think of something," said Snowy. They both giggled. This should be fun. All of a sudden Snowy jumped up. "I know!" he exclaimed. "Snow White and the Seven Dwarfs." "But there are only two of us," said Bradley. "I know," Snowy replied, "but some of the little bears in the village shop window would love to come."

Lunch forgotten, the two bears raced to the village and into the shop selling bears. Both bears were talking at the same time. "Slow down," said the shopkeeper, "and tell me what you are talking about!" "Well we have had a wonderful idea for this afternoon's competition. We are sure you will want to help." When they had explained, the shopkeeper laughed. "You are going to need a dress and headscarf, Snowy, but I think I can find something. Bradley and six small bears need matching trousers and waistcoats." All the bears in the window started to get very excited. "Can we come? Oh please let us." The shopkeeper chose six small bears and they all dressed up. The bigger bears looked very sad and one started to growl. Bradley asked the shopkeeper as it was to be such a special day if all the other bears could come and watch. And so it was that the shop closed and all the bears went onto the Green.

Snowy and Bradley put their names down to enter the competition. They were told the event would be at 3 o'clock. "We have plenty of time to watch the dancing. Come on," said Bradley. The music was playing, the bears were singing. Everyone seemed happy, until they came to the Dancing Round the Maypole. There all the children were crying. "Whatever is the matter?" asked Bradley. "Two of the children who were to dance are not feeling very well," the teacher said. Bradley and Snowy looked at each other. "We can dance," they said. The children cheered. Teacher said, "it is not as easy as it looks, but you can try." "We'll help them," the children said. "All right. Music please." Oh how they danced. The children had to guide them a little bit and now and again the ribbons became tangled. No–one seemed to mind, and everyone finished in the correct place.

The people watching cheered and clapped and the May Queen gave Bradley and Snowy a hug and kiss. Snowy was quite embarrassed and turned a little pink! The two ran off to take part in the Fancy Dress Competition. A great number of children had entered. There was Spiderman, Clowns, Ballet Dancers, Barbie Dolls and Batman, even a dog in a pram wearing a bonnet. They all had to stand in a line to be judged. The bears could hardly keep still they were so excited. They did look smart in their green suits, each carrying a small spade over their shoulder. Then they started to sing the Snow White song. "Hi! Ho!, Hi! Ho!, it's off to work we go," which made everyone laugh and clap. The judges said, "Well after that effort Snow White and the Seven Dwarfs deserve First Prize."

Snowy, Bradley and the other dwarfs jumped for joy. First prize was a return ticket on the Hurst Castle Ferry from Keyhaven for all of them. "We will have a wonderful time," said Bradley. And they did. But that's another story.

Bradley in his "Going out" clothes.

Story 3 Bradley's Party at Hurst Castle

Bradley the little grey New Forest bear was staying at Milford-on-Sea with his friend Snowy. They, with six other little bears had won the Fancy Dress Competition as Snow White and the Seven Dwarfs. The prize was a return ticket for all of them to Hurst Castle on the Ferry from Keyhaven. Bradley knew the weather was going to be perfect. "Shall we have a Beach Party?" he asked Snowy. "Great idea," said Snowy. "We must ask all the other bears to come. It will be a wonderful party."

The day dawned bright and clear. All the bears gathered together on the Village Green at Milford. Through the car park and along the gravel path they marched, over the wooden bridge and past Sturt Pond. Soon they came to Keyhaven. The Captain of the Ferry saw them coming and welcomed them aboard.

The Ferry's engine started. Out of the harbour they went, past the mud flats and on down the river. They soon arrived at Hurst Castle and ran up from the beach onto the grass. "We'll put all the food and drink in the shade of the Castle wall," said Bradley wisely, "to keep it cool." "What shall we play first?" asked one of the smaller bears. "Rounders would be fun," said another. Bradley quickly found the bat and ball. They divided into two teams. Bradley's team were first to bat and Snowy's to bowl and field. When it came to Bradley's turn he hit the ball very hard and down onto the beach it went. All the bears ran after it.

When they reached the beach they all started to shout at once. "Bradley, come quickly, do." There, much to Bradley's horror, he could see a boat with two people on board drifting helplessly in the fast flowing water. The people shouted to Bradley. "Help us, our boat is sinking." Bradley shouted back, "I'll call the Coastguard." He started running towards the Castle. He knocked at the door and quickly explained what was wrong. The Gatekeeper telephoned for the Coastguard who called the Lifeboat. Bradley ran back to the beach. Very soon they saw the orange Lifeboat in the distance, coming very fast towards them. Bradley and Snowy moved all the young bears out of the way where they would be safe. Just then the Coastguard came down the track with the siren screaming and blue lights flashing.

The Coastguard watched through his binoculars as the Lifeboat crew threw a rope to the people on the sinking boat. They tied the rope on securely. The Lifeboat came alongside and lifted the people to safety aboard the Lifeboat. And so they were rescued. The Lifeboat came close into the shore and the rescued people called out thanks to Bradley. The Coastguard came over to the group of bears and said, "Well done all of you! Not only did you call for help immediately but you did not put yourselves in danger by getting in the way. Now all of you, come with me to the Castle. Free tickets to enter and free ice creams for all of you."

And so it was that the bears had their party in the Castle and were able to explore. Up and down little staircases they went calling to each other, laughing and pretending that they were kings and soldiers commanding great armies. When they were exhausted they ran down onto the lawn in front of the Castle. They sat in a circle enjoying their party and free ice cream.

Later that day, a very tired group of bears made their way home. What an exciting day they had and what a story to tell.

Bradley

Colour me in on Page 2.

Page 18